THE SECRET OF THE SWORDS

SWORD GIRL

THE SECRET OF THE Swords

FRANCES WATTS

ILLUSTRATED BY GREGORY ROGERS

ALLEN&UNWIN

First published in 2012

Allen & Unwin
83 Alexander Street
Crows Nest NSW 2065
Australia
Phone: (61 2) 8425 0100
Fax: (61 2) 9906 2218
Email: info@allenandunwin.com
Web: www.allenandunwin.com

A Cataloguing-in-Publication entry is available from the National
Library of Australia
www.trove.nla.gov.au

ISBN 978 1 74237 728 5

Cover design by Seymour Designs
Cover illustration by Gregory Rogers
Text design by Seymour Designs
Set in 16/21 pt Adobe Jenson Pro by Seymour Designs
This book was printed in February 2015 at Griffin Press,
168 Cross Keys Road, Salisbury South SA 5106.

10 9 8 7 6

MIX
Paper from
responsible sources
FSC® C009448
www.fsc.org

The paper in this book is FSC® certified.
FSC® promotes environmentally responsible,
socially beneficial and economically viable
management of the world's forests.

For Dad, who brings history alive

F. W.

For Matt

G. R.

CHAPTER 1

'THOMASINA?'

Tommy ignored the voice calling her. 'Go, Sir Benedict!' she whispered.

'Thomasina!'

Tommy knew it would be Mrs Moon, the cook, angry because she wasn't standing at the long table peeling mountains of potatoes with the other kitchen girls. Instead, Tommy was standing at the kitchen

doorway, watching the knights practising in the great courtyard.

Clank, clank. The courtyard rang with the sound of sword against armour.

Sir Benedict and another knight, Sir Hugh, were teaching the squires how to fight.

'Now I thrust,' Sir Benedict called. He lunged forward with his sword.

Sir Hugh then drove his sword at Sir Benedict.

'Now I parry,' Sir Benedict explained, as he blocked the blow with his own sword.

The squires, who were boys training to be knights, copied Sir Benedict's moves with their wooden practice swords. So did Tommy, with the small paring knife she was meant to be using on the potatoes.

'Hooray!' Tommy cheered softly as Sir Benedict, Flamant Castle's bravest knight, raised his sword to signal the end of practice. The sun glinted off the steel blade, and for a moment Tommy imagined that she was the one holding her sword aloft. That she was the castle's most daring knight, its most skilled sword fighter.

'Ouch!' Tommy cried, as a hand grasped her ear and twisted it hard.

'So there you are, Thomasina,' Mrs Moon scolded. 'I should have known you'd be watching the knights again. You're meant to be peeling potatoes, not dreaming in doorways.'

'Sorry, Mrs Moon,' Tommy murmured. She turned to follow the cook back into the gloomy kitchen with its smoke-blackened stone walls.

But Mrs Moon blocked her way. 'Not so fast, girl. I've got another job for you. Since you clearly prefer the courtyard to the kitchen, you can sweep it.' She thrust a broom at Tommy.

Tommy gaped at the cook in astonishment. 'Sweep the whole courtyard? But the courtyard is huge! It will take me forever!'

'You'd best get started then,' Mrs Moon said.

With a sigh, Tommy took the broom. As the knights led the squires away, she trudged across the flagstones to the far side of the courtyard. The castle walls and towers reared high above her, and she could just see the guards keeping lookout from the battlements.

'I bet those guards don't care whether the courtyard is dusty,' Tommy grumbled to herself as she began to sweep. 'And I bet the knights don't either. They're worried about more important things, like keeping Sir Walter's castle and lands safe.' Flamant Castle belonged to Sir Walter the Bald and his wife, Lady Beatrix the Bored.

Tommy was so busy grumbling that she didn't notice what was going on nearby until she heard an indignant yowl.

Looking up, she saw a stocky boy with bright red hair. Tommy had seen him before, though she had never spoken to him. He was one of the boys who worked in the armoury, where all the weapons and armour were repaired and stored.

'Don't know what he's got to yowl about,'

Tommy muttered. 'He gets to spend all day with the swords and bows while I'm scrubbing pots in the scullery and chopping vegetables in the kitchen.'

Her thoughts were interrupted by another yowl, and then a low hiss.

Tommy pushed her mop of hair out of her eyes and looked at the boy again. This time she noticed that he was holding one of the wooden practice swords. He was jabbing the tip of the sword at a black and white cat he'd trapped in a corner, and it was the cat who was yowling.

'Hey!' Tommy called. 'You leave that cat alone.'

The red-haired boy turned around. 'Who's going to make me?' he sneered. 'You?' He jabbed the cat again.

This time the cat mewed

pitifully and Tommy, who loved animals, ran towards the pair.

'Stop!' she cried. 'You're hurting it.'

The boy spun around and pointed the sword at Tommy. 'Who are you?' he demanded.

'I'm – I'm Tommy. I work in the kitchen.'

'A kitchen girl?' said the boy. He laughed rudely. 'Well I don't take orders from kitchen girls – I'm Keeper of the Bows. I'm in charge of all the castle's crossbows and longbows. What are you in charge of?' His gaze fell on the broom Tommy was still holding in one hand. 'Ha! I know – you're Keeper of the Brooms!' He snorted with laughter at his own joke, then said, 'Go away, kitchen girl, I'm practising my sword fighting.'

He turned and lunged towards the cat. Tommy sprang forward and with her free hand grabbed the hem of his tunic.

With an angry shout the boy pushed

Tommy away roughly. 'Would you rather I practise on you?' he said.

'At least it would be a fair fight,' Tommy snapped.

'A fair fight?' scoffed the boy. 'How dare you presume to be my equal! Get lost, kitchen girl.' And then he lifted his sword above his head and spun on his heel.

As the wooden blade tore through the air towards the cat cowering against the stones, Tommy leaped forward. Flinging herself between the boy and the cat, she halted the sword's arc with the broomstick.

'I warned you!' he snarled, before swinging his arm back and driving his blade straight at Tommy.

CHAPTER 2

TOMMY'S HEART was pounding as she dodged to her left. The point of the wooden sword snagged on the thin fabric of her dress, tearing it.

The boy lunged at her again, and again Tommy dodged.

'Don't you know how to do anything but dodge?' the boy jeered. 'You might have a boy's name, but you fight like a girl!'

Tommy's fear turned to outrage. How dare he? First he was rude to her because she worked in the kitchen, now he thought he was better than her just because he was a boy!

He swung the sword again, and suddenly a voice in Tommy's head said, 'Parry!' She lifted her broom to block him.

Taken by surprise, the boy nearly lost his balance. He glared at Tommy and began to lash out wildly with the wooden sword, slashing the air this way and that.

Tommy, without even thinking, parried every blow. It was as if her arm was remembering all the times she had watched the knights with their swords, and knew exactly what to do.

By now the boy was panting and his face was as red as his hair. His movements were growing slow and clumsy, but Tommy, who was smaller and lighter, felt full of energy.

'Come on,' she said, holding the broomstick in both hands and waving it back and forth. 'You can beat a kitchen girl with a broom, can't you?'

The boy's grip tightened on his sword. 'I'll show you ...' he began, but before he could show her anything a shout rang across the courtyard.

'Reynard! Get in here at once!'

The boy let his sword fall to his side. 'Coming, Smith!' he called over his shoulder. Looking at Tommy, he narrowed his eyes and said, 'You're in big trouble, kitchen girl.'

Then he turned and hurried towards the armoury.

Tommy sighed. The boy – Reynard – was right. What had she been thinking? She, a mere kitchen girl, fighting the Keeper of the Bows! 'I *am* in big trouble,' she said aloud.

'I wouldn't be so sure,' said a voice.

Tommy jumped. 'Who said that?' She looked around the courtyard. It was deserted. Perhaps a guard …? But when she looked up to the tops of the towers, shading her eyes against the sun, the guards all had their backs to her.

She turned to look at the cat, which was now calmly licking its paw. The cat paused in its licking to meet Tommy's gaze, then returned to its bath.

Tommy shrugged. She must have imagined the voice. Just as she had imagined her broom was a wooden sword, like Reynard's. She looked at the broom, which she still grasped in both hands. Reynard could practise with his wooden sword and one day become a squire. Tommy could practise with her broom as much as she liked, but she would still only be a kitchen girl. It was time she gave up her impossible dreams of becoming a knight, of fighting battles and winning tournaments. She should be dreaming proper kitchen-girl dreams, of growing up and becoming … a cook. Lowering the broom to the ground, she began to sweep.

Behind her, the cat finished its bath, stretched, and walked away.

The sun had sunk below the battlements when Tommy returned to the kitchen. Her arms ached from the constant motion of sweeping, and even when she closed her eyes from weariness she could still see the endless rows of flagstones. All she wanted was a bowl of soup then to fall into bed, but Mrs Moon had other ideas. She wanted to scold Tommy some more.

'Now I hope you've learned your lesson, Thomasina,' the cook began. 'And there'll be no more of this nonsense about—'

'Ah, excuse me.' In the doorway stood a man so tall his dark hair nearly brushed the top of the doorframe.

'Sir Benedict!' Mrs Moon exclaimed. 'Goodness me, what brings you to the kitchen, sir?'

'I'm looking for one of your kitchen girls,' said the knight. 'Her name is Tommy, I believe. I hear she had a bit of bother with one of the boys from the armoury.'

Tommy looked at the floor in dismay. She never should have fought that horrible Reynard!

'Thomasina!' Mrs Moon's voice was shrill. 'What have you been up to, girl?'

Sir Benedict turned to Tommy. 'I've been told you like to watch the knights practise.'

Tommy blushed but didn't say anything. Had someone been watching her while she was watching the knights?

'And I hear you know how to handle a sword,' Sir Benedict continued. 'Or a broom, rather.' His blue eyes twinkled.

'I love swords, sir,' Tommy blurted out. 'Much more than brooms,' she added.

Mrs Moon said tartly, 'That's no use to me in the kitchen, girl. I'd rather you knew how to handle a paring knife.'

'You are quite right,' the knight said. 'Tommy is no use in the kitchen.'

Oh no! Did Sir Benedict mean to throw her out of the castle? But she had nowhere else to go! No family, no home. Flamant Castle was her only home.

'That is why,' Sir Benedict continued,

'I would like to offer Tommy a job in the armoury.'

Tommy's mouth dropped open. 'In the armoury, sir?' she whispered.

Sir Benedict nodded. 'That's right. One of the boys, Edward, has become a squire, so I am looking for someone to take his place. Edward looked after all the bladed weapons: the swords and daggers. What do you say, Tommy? Will you be the castle's new Keeper of the Blades?'

CHAPTER 3

THE KEEPER of the Blades ... Tommy was swelling with pride as she walked across the courtyard to the armoury the next morning, ready to start her new job.

Even Mrs Moon had been impressed that Sir Benedict himself had come to the kitchen. After the knight had left, she filled a bowl with hearty bean soup for Tommy. And even better, she gave Tommy a tunic and a pair of leggings that her son had outgrown. 'Much more suitable for a Keeper of the Blades than a torn dress,' the cook had remarked.

When she entered the armoury, the first thing Tommy noticed was the noise. The blacksmith was bent over a sturdy wooden bench, hammering a large sheet of metal. The sound echoed off the stone walls, which glowed with the light from the fireplace set against the back wall.

As her eyes had adjusted to the dim light, Tommy looked around. She saw an assortment of shields and breastplates, helmets and swords, all waiting for repair.

When the blacksmith paused in his hammering, Tommy stepped forward.

'Good morning, sir,' she said. 'I'm Tommy, the new Keeper of the Blades.'

The blacksmith straightened up and squinted at her from under a pair of big bushy eyebrows. 'So you're the new sword girl, eh? Well you can drop the "sir" and just call me Smith. Everyone does. Right then, I'll show you what's what.' Smith beckoned for Tommy to follow him.

'That's the forge,' he said, pointing to the fireplace. 'If we need to reshape a piece of armour we put it in the fire there. The heat softens it so we can bend it easily. We only do repairs here, though. The weapons and armour are made by the smiths in town.'

Tommy felt a prickle of excitement. She knew that many of the castle's needs were supplied by the merchants and tradesmen

in the town just outside the castle's walls. Most days, the drawbridge across the moat was busy with carts and horses going back and forth between the castle and the town. As a kitchen girl, Tommy had hardly ever visited the town. But maybe as the Keeper of the Blades she would!

There were doors on either side of the forge. Smith led Tommy to the door on the left. 'This is the sword chamber,' he said. 'First time we've had a girl in the job that I can remember. But I suppose Sir Benedict knows what he's about.'

Tommy stood in the doorway of the low-ceilinged room. There were no windows, but the light from a candle on the wall to the right of the door was reflected in the gleaming blades lining three walls of the long, narrow chamber. Tommy thought she had never seen a more beautiful sight

The long wall facing her was lined with swords standing in wooden racks, and in the shadows to her left she could just make out a smaller rack of swords. To her right, daggers hung by their hilts from iron pegs which had been hammered into the stone wall.

'You're to keep the blades polished and sharp, ready for the knights. You've got plenty of cloths here and a pot of oil for polishing, and there's your file and whetstone for sharpening. If any repairs are needed, you bring 'em to me. Simple enough, eh, Sword Girl?'

'Yes, Smith,' Tommy breathed, without taking her eyes from the dazzling array of swords.

As soon as the blacksmith left the room and she could hear the muffled clang of his hammer, Tommy pulled a sword from the long rack. It was so much heavier than a broom, but she liked the weight of it. She liked the way the steel blade sliced the air, liked the smooth feel of the wooden grip.

She had just replaced the sword in its rack when the hammering in the armoury stopped. 'You're late,' Smith said gruffly.

'Never mind that,' said a familiar voice. 'Has Sir Benedict been in? Did he say anything about making me Keeper of the Blades?'

It was Reynard, Tommy realised. But what did he mean about Sir Benedict making *him* Keeper of the Blades? She stepped closer to the door to listen.

'Sir Benedict didn't say nothin' about you bein' Keeper of the Blades, lad,' the blacksmith replied. 'The new sword girl is already here.'

'Sword girl? What are you talking about, Smith?'

'See for yourself,' said Smith.

And before Tommy could move away from the doorway Reynard was there, his red hair coppery in the candlelight.

'You!' he cried. He turned to call over his shoulder, 'She isn't a Keeper of the Blades, Smith. She's just a kitchen girl.'

'Not according to Sir Benedict,' said the

blacksmith calmly. 'He reckons she's the sword girl, and if Sir Benedict reckons it, then it must be so.'

Reynard turned to glare at Tommy. He seemed to be vibrating with anger as he said in a menacing whisper, 'We'll see about that.'

CHAPTER 4

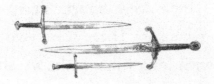

THE KEEPER of the Bows stormed off. Tommy guessed the bow chamber must be through the door to the right of the forge.

She was feeling a bit upset by Reynard's final words. Was he really threatening her? Well, Tommy thought, she would just have to look after the swords and daggers so well that there would be no question of giving her job to someone else.

She would begin by getting to know the swords, starting with the long rack, she decided. She knew from watching the knights that there were different kinds of swords. There were short, sharp-pointed thrusting swords. There were two-handed swords with long hilts, so heavy she could hardly lift them. There were double-edged swords with broad blades. She wiped each one with a soft cloth and clove-scented oil.

Halfway along the wall, she pulled a sword from the rack that made her draw in her breath in awe. Studded with rubies at the hilt, its blade was decorated with exquisite engravings of flamingos, matching the birds on the flags that fluttered from the towers of Flamant Castle. It was so precious she didn't dare wave it about like she had with some of the other swords. After admiring it for a few minutes, she polished it with special care, then put it back in the rack and continued her inspection.

When she had finished with the main rack, she turned to the small collection of swords along the short wall. She was puzzled to find that the swords here were nowhere near as well cared for as the others. The blades were dull and tarnished, and the wooden grips were as worn as the handle on the kitchen broom.

The thought of the old broom reminded her of Reynard's words from the day before.

'Keeper of the Brooms,' he had called her. She smiled to think how her life had changed in only one day. From Keeper of the Brooms to Keeper of the Blades! 'But how did Sir Benedict know that I could handle swords?' she wondered aloud. 'How did he find out about me and the broom?'

'That's easy,' said a voice behind her. 'I told him.'

Tommy gasped and spun around. At first she didn't see anyone, but then a movement below made her drop her gaze. At her feet was the black and white cat.

'You – you told him?' she repeated. Surely the cat hadn't spoken – but there was no one else in the room.

'I did,' said the cat. 'I told Sir Benedict how you fought off that oaf Reynard with

only a broom. I also told him how much you love to watch the knights practising in the courtyard.'

'You know about that?' Tommy asked.

'I know most things that go on in Flamant Castle,' the cat told her. 'So how do you like your new job so far?'

'I love it!' said Tommy. 'There are so many beautiful swords in here. Like that one with the rubies.' She pointed to the main rack.

'That's Sir Walter the Bald's sword,' the cat said. 'He's very proud of it, so mind you keep it sharp and well polished. He likes to come and check on it.'

'Sir Walter comes in here?' said Tommy. She thought she might die of nerves if he did. Lady Beatrix had visited the kitchen now and then to speak to Mrs Moon. But

no one from the kitchen had ever met Sir Walter.

'Why are the swords over there so dusty?' Tommy asked, pointing to the smaller rack.

'Ah, you mean the Old Wrecks,' said the cat.

'I don't think they're wrecks at all,' Tommy protested. 'They just need to be looked after properly and they'll be as fine as all the other swords.'

'You're absolutely right,' said the cat. She sounded pleased. 'I think you'll do well here.'

'Thank you, um, cat,' said Tommy. 'And thank you for telling Sir Benedict about me.'

'Lil,' said the cat. 'My name is Lil. And

you're welcome, Tommy.' Then, with her tail in the air, Lil strolled out of the chamber as silently as she had entered.

'A talking cat,' Tommy said to herself. 'Did that really happen or did I imagine it?'

She shrugged, picked up a cloth and approached the Old Wrecks. 'I don't know why you've just been abandoned,' she murmured as she pulled a sabre from the rack and began to polish it.

'You see?' said the sabre. 'I told you a sword girl was a fine idea.'

CHAPTER 5

Tommy screamed and dropped the sabre to the floor. There was a clatter of steel on stone, and Smith appeared in the doorway.

'Is there a problem, Sword Girl?' he asked.

'No, I'm – I'm fine, thank you, Smith,' Tommy said.

The blacksmith looked from Tommy to the sabre on the floor. 'What's that you're doing? Polishing the Old Wrecks? You needn't bother with that. The knights never use that lot. They only like new swords, or swords that have been carried into battle. None of those ever 'as been.' He stumped away.

When she was sure he was out of earshot, Tommy picked up the sabre with trembling hands. First a talking cat, and now the swords were talking. Could her mind be playing tricks on her? Perhaps she had sunstroke from the hours she'd spent sweeping the courtyard the day before. Yes, that must be it. But just to be sure she took a deep breath and said, 'I'm sorry. Did you ... did you say something?'

'I was just telling Bevan Brumm over there that I was right,' said the sabre. It was a woman's voice. 'He said a sword girl was

a silly idea, but I told him he didn't know what he was talking about. So will you admit I was right now, Bevan Brumm?'

'It is possible you were not wrong,' came a deep voice from the rack of Old Wrecks.

'Well I suppose that's as good as I'll get from you,' the sabre said.

'Excuse me,' said Tommy, whose head was still whirling. 'This is real, isn't it? You're … you're talking.'

'Yes, thank you for letting us know,' said the voice of Bevan Brumm. He sounded sarcastic, Tommy thought. 'She's a bit slow, your sword girl, Nursie.'

Tommy opened her mouth to argue, but a third voice beat her to it.

'She's not slow, Bevan.' It was a boy's voice. 'She's probably just surprised. I'll bet when you were alive, you would have been surprised if a sword started talking.'

'It is possible you are not wrong,' said Bevan stiffly.

'There he goes again,' said Nursie.

'Sword Girl,' said the boy, 'my name is Jasper Swann.'

Tommy looked at the sword with the boy's voice. It was slender, slightly curved with a pointed blade. 'Are you a ghost, Jasper?' Tommy asked in a quavering voice.

'I suppose I am,' said Jasper. 'But I can't walk through walls or anything like that. I was a squire, but I fell ill before I had

the chance to fight in a single battle. Since then, my spirit has inhabited my sword, which I was holding when I died.'

'I was a merchant,' a long-handled dagger said. This was Bevan Brumm. 'I was travelling through a forest when I was set upon by bandits. I pulled my dagger from my cloak, but I was too late.'

'I was a nursemaid,' said Nursie. 'I was looking after the children when the castle was attacked. I used this sword to fight off the enemy who tried to snatch my little darlings. I saved the children, but I wasn't so lucky myself.'

Tommy waved her hand at the rest of the Old Wrecks in the rack. 'What about the others? Are they ... like you?'

'The rest of them sleep most of the time,' said Bevan Brumm disapprovingly. 'But yes, we all died with our weapons in our hands.'

'Oh! That's so sad,' Tommy burst out.

Nursie laughed. 'There, there, dear. It all happened a long time ago. We're long past feeling sorry for ourselves.'

Still, Tommy wished there was something she could do. 'Would you like me to polish you?' she asked shyly.

'That would be lovely,' said Nursie.

So Tommy polished Nursie till her blade shone, then did the same for Bevan Brumm. Finally, she lifted Jasper Swann from the rack. He was surprisingly light compared to the other swords she had lifted that day, and the narrow grip felt just right in her hand.

'Go on,' Jasper urged. 'Try me out.'

Hesitantly at first, then with more confidence, Tommy wielded the sword, slashing and slicing the air.

'Good,' said Jasper. 'But when you're fighting, don't face your enemy. You should stand side on. That way less of your body is exposed to his sword.'

'I see,' said Tommy. She adjusted her position and did another few thrusts and parries.

Jasper said, 'That's it!'

'Well done,' Bevan Brumm agreed.

'You stick with us, dearie,' Nursie told

her, 'and we'll help you become the castle's finest sword fighter. After all our years in here, there's not much we can't tell you about swords. Who knows? Maybe you'll become the first-ever girl squire!'

The first-ever girl squire! Nursie's words were still ringing in her ears as Tommy sprang from her bed early the next morning. Sir Benedict and Mrs Moon had decided that Tommy should continue to share sleeping quarters and take her meals with the kitchen girls rather than sleep in the barracks as the last Keeper of the Blades had done.

Tommy quickly ate a piece of bread, then

crossed the courtyard to the armoury, eager to get to work. Today she was planning to check the blade of every sword for sharpness.

But the minute Tommy stepped into the sword chamber her plans were forgotten, as the Old Wrecks started clamouring.

'Sword Girl! Sword Girl! Thank goodness you've come. Sir Walter was here at dawn!'

Tommy's throat went dry. 'Was he happy with his sword?' she asked in a voice barely louder than a whisper.

'He was not,' boomed Bevan Brumm.

Tommy clapped a hand over her mouth. What had she done wrong?

'He wasn't unhappy with your work, dearie,' Nursie explained.

Tommy shook her head in confusion. 'Then what …?' she began.

'His sword wasn't here,' said Jasper.

'Wasn't here?' Tommy thought she must have misheard. 'Where was it?'

'It's gone,' Bevan Brumm announced. 'Disappeared. Vanished. Lost without a trace.'

'I'm sorry, Tommy,' said Jasper. 'Sir Walter's sword has been stolen.'

CHAPTER 6

'STOLEN?' Tommy gasped. 'But that's impossible! Who would steal Sir Walter's sword?'

'We don't know, dearie,' said Nursie. 'It must have happened in the middle of the night when we were asleep.'

Tommy hardly dared ask her next question. 'What did Sir Walter say when he couldn't find his sword? Did he ... did he say anything about me?'

'He demanded to know where the Keeper of the Blades was, but Nursie managed to put him off,' said Bevan with a chuckle.

'He'll be back though,' said Nursie. 'You'd better find that sword in a jiffy or not even Sir Benedict will be able to save your job.'

'But I don't even know where to start,' said Tommy desperately.

'Why don't you ask Lil?' said Jasper. 'She knows everything that goes on around the castle.'

'Yes!' said Tommy. 'That's a great idea.' She raced through the armoury and out into the courtyard.

The castle was just starting to stir, and the courtyard was coming to life.

Chambermaids were gossiping as they aired their mistresses' sheets, a groom was leading a messenger's horse to the stables and masons were busy repairing a section of stone wall. But where was Lil?

Tommy scanned the courtyard anxiously, at last spotting the black and white cat stretched out in a puddle of sunshine, observing the goings-on around her.

Tommy ran over. 'Lil,' she said, 'you have to help me. Please.'

The cat turned her watchful green eyes on the sword girl. 'What's wrong, Tommy?'

'Someone has stolen Sir Walter's sword,' Tommy told her. 'And if I don't find it quickly, I'll be sent back to the kitchen!' She gulped. Maybe she'd even be forced to leave Flamant Castle!

Lil sprang to her feet. 'We'll see about that.'

We'll see about that ... The words sent a shiver down Tommy's spine. They were the same words Reynard had used when he found out that Tommy was the new sword girl.

'Lil,' said Tommy, 'I think Reynard, the Keeper of the Bows, might have taken it. He wanted the job of Keeper of the Blades for himself.'

'That oaf?' said the cat scornfully. 'Not if I have anything to do with it.'

She lifted a paw to stroke her whiskers thoughtfully. 'What we need is a bird's-eye view,' she said.

'Do you mean we should climb one of the towers?' said Tommy. 'It might be a bit hard to see the sword from up there.'

'That won't be necessary,' said Lil. 'We'll ask the bird's-eye view to come to us.' She tilted her head towards the sky. 'Pigeon,' she called. 'Are you there?'

A few moments later, there was a flutter of feathers as a plump grey pigeon landed on a flagstone beside them.

'Not so loud,' the pigeon muttered. 'I'm hiding.'

'Is the physician after you again?' Lil asked as Tommy stared at the talking bird. Did every creature at the castle talk? Why

had she never known this before?

The pigeon sighed. 'Yes, he wants my droppings for one of his potions.' The bird stuck his chest out. 'I am a carrier pigeon,' he declared. 'I carry important messages. It is insulting to be hounded for my droppings.'

'Quite,' said Lil, and it seemed to Tommy that the cat was trying not to smile. 'Pigeon, I know you're a bit of a night owl,' she continued, 'and you like to keep an eagle – I mean a *pigeon* eye on the castle. I was wondering if you saw anything unusual around the armoury last night. Perhaps someone sneaking out with a sword?'

'Why, I did see someone with a sword last night,' said the pigeon. 'It was that nasty boy who tried to shoot me down with a slingshot last week.'

Tommy and Lil exchanged glances. 'That sounds like Reynard,' Tommy said.

'Yes, yes,' said the pigeon. 'That's him. Reynard. He ran out of the armoury, and I remember being glad that he was holding a sword and not a slingshot. There's no way he could reach me with a sword, I thought. He climbed to the top of the south tower and, when the guard wasn't looking, he threw the sword over the battlements and into the moat.'

Tommy buried her face in her hands. 'Not the moat,' she moaned. 'It's patrolled by a crocodile. We'll never get the sword back.'

'Actually,' said Lil, but she was interrupted by a squawk as the pigeon abruptly took off

in a flurry of feathers. The next minute, Tommy was almost knocked over when someone barged into her from behind.

'What—?' she started. She turned to see a short round man in a brown robe. His gaze was fixed on the sky.

'It's the physician,' Lil said in a low voice.

'Where is that pigeon?' the physician was saying to himself. 'Sir Walter the Bald is suffering and is in need of a cure.'

'What's wrong with Sir Walter?' asked Tommy. The Old Wrecks hadn't mentioned that he was ill.

'Mental confusion,' said the physician. 'Poor Sir Walter. He was in the sword chamber very early this morning, checking on his favourite sword, when he thought he heard his old nurse's voice telling him to hurry back to bed, dearie, and don't make a fuss. Of course, it was all in his head. Sir Walter's nurse died some fifty years ago.'

'Nursie!' Tommy said, realising one of Nursie's 'little darlings' must have been Sir Walter the Bald.

The physician gave her a puzzled look. 'Are you suffering from mental confusion too, girl?'

'No,' Tommy assured him.

'Anyway,' the physician continued, 'the most effective cure for mental confusion is to mix pigeon droppings with honey, and apply the mixture to the back of the patient's neck. Now where is that pigeon?' The physician lifted his gaze to the sky once more, and wandered off across the courtyard.

'Quick,' said Lil. 'This way.'

Tommy followed Lil under the low arch leading out of the courtyard and through the castle gate. Once outside the walls, they ran to the edge of the moat.

Looking down into the murky water, Tommy knew it was hopeless. There was no way they'd be able to spot the sword in the sluggish, weed-choked water of the moat encircling the castle. And even if they did spot it, there was still the matter of the—

'Aaaaah!' Tommy screamed in terror as a hideous beast emerged from the water, its enormous jaws open wide to reveal two jagged rows of sharp teeth. 'Crocodile!'

CHAPTER 7

'REALLY, CROC,' said Lil. 'How many times do I have to tell you to cover your mouth when you yawn?'

'Sorry,' said the crocodile. He swam closer to the edge of the moat, where Tommy was kneeling, frozen to the spot. After a sly glance at Lil, he opened his mouth again. '*Muuuuuurp.*'

'*And* when you burp,' the cat added

sternly. 'You'll make a bad impression on our new sword girl.'

'She started it.' The giant reptile sounded sulky. 'She called me a crocodile.'

Tommy didn't understand. 'But aren't you a crocodile?'

'I'm a croco*diddle*,' he sniffed. 'There's a difference, you know.'

'I didn't know,' Tommy said. 'What's a crocodiddle?'

'Me,' said the crocodiddle, as if that settled it. 'What do you want, anyway?'

Lil explained about the sword and the crocodiddle's beady yellow eyes lit up. 'So that's whose it is! I was just doing a couple of laps in the middle of the night – backstroke, butterfly, that kind of thing – when a sword splashed into the water right behind me. It almost sliced off my tail!'

'Do you think you could find it, Mr Crocodiddle?' Tommy asked. 'Please?'

The crocodiddle tilted his head to one side. 'Did you hear that?' he asked Lil in a loud whisper. 'She called me "mister".' He turned back to Tommy. 'I'll see if I can, young Sword Girl.' He gave her a wide, toothy grin and swam off.

Several minutes passed, then several minutes more, but the crocodiddle didn't return. Tommy's throat felt tight. That was it then. The sword was lost forever at the bottom of the moat. She would be sent back to the kitchen in disgrace. Or worse, she'd be—

Suddenly the surface of the water began

to shiver. Two yellow eyes appeared, then an ugly snout. And there, clasped delicately between the crocodiddle's pointy teeth, was Sir Walter's sword. It was draped with weeds but seemed otherwise unharmed.

'Oh, thank you,' Tommy cried as she took the sword from the crocodiddle's jaws. 'Thank you!'

'Now run,' Lil urged. 'Get the sword cleaned up and back in the rack before Sir Walter recovers from his mental confusion.'

Tommy didn't need to be told twice. She sprinted back to the castle gate, squeezed past a cart full of hay that was almost blocking the entrance to the castle, then pelted across the courtyard to the armoury.

Inside, all was quiet.

Smith looked up from the helmet he was

repairing. 'Everything all right, Sword Girl?'

'Yes, thank you, Smith,' Tommy replied. 'It is now.'

With Sir Walter's dripping sword in her hand, Tommy stalked past the blacksmith to the door of the bow chamber. She could see Reynard sharpening a steel-tipped arrow.

'What do you want?' he said when he spotted Tommy in the doorway. Then he saw Sir Walter's sword in her hand and turned pale. 'How did ...? Where did you ...?' he stammered.

'You know where I found it,' said Tommy coldly. 'In the moat, where you threw it.'

'You can't prove it was me,' Reynard argued, but he sounded scared.

'I can prove it,' said Tommy. 'I have a

witness who saw you do it. And if you touch
any of my swords again, I'll tell Sir Benedict
what you did to Sir Walter's sword. Then
we'll see who's Keeper of the Brooms.'

Back in the sword chamber the Old

Wrecks were overjoyed to see Tommy with Sir Walter's sword. As she wiped the weeds from the engraved blade, she told them how the sword had come to be at the bottom of the moat. Soon the blade shone a brilliant silver once more.

'Look how nicely she's cleaned it,' Nursie remarked.

'She does have a way with swords,' Bevan Brumm agreed.

Jasper said, 'I think she's the best Keeper of the Blades since ...'

But he didn't finish the sentence, falling silent at the sound of a sharp voice saying, 'Morning, Smith. Is that new sword girl here? I want to check on my sword.'

'Yes, Sir Walter, sir. She's in the chamber.'

Tommy hastily put her cloths away then

stood on the cold stone floor, holding the sword.

'Sword Girl? Where's my – oh, there it is.'

Tommy had her head bowed, but she peeked up as Sir Walter the Bald took his sword from her outstretched hands. She held her breath as he examined his sword from every angle.

'Good day, Sir Walter.' Sir Benedict entered the chamber, accompanied by Lil.

Sir Walter turned to face the new arrivals, his face glowing. 'Sir Benedict! Doesn't my sword look particularly marvellous today? Very pleasing, Sword Girl. Very pleasing indeed.' He nodded once, slid his sword back into the centre of the main rack, and left the room. Tommy wasn't sure, but she thought she saw a few smears of something

sticky on the back of his neck. She smiled to herself. Sir Walter probably thought the physician's mixture had worked. How surprised he would be to know that he hadn't been suffering from mental confusion at all – his old nurse really had spoken to him!

'Dear little Walter, he hasn't changed a bit,' said Nursie fondly. 'And he certainly seems to approve of our sword girl.'

'And so he should,' said Bevan Brumm. 'She's just like that excellent sword boy we had, oh, about twenty years ago. He polished us and sharpened us and saw to it that we were never neglected.'

'Exactly,' Jasper broke in. 'She's the best Keeper of the Blades since ...' Again, he trailed off.

'Since who?' Tommy demanded.

'Yes, since who?' said Sir Benedict. He sounded amused.

Jasper gave an embarrassed laugh. 'Since you, sir.'

'Thank you, Jasper Swann,' said Sir Benedict. 'You're very kind.'

Tommy looked up at Sir Benedict. 'You were a Keeper of the Blades, sir?' she asked. 'Like me?'

Sir Benedict smiled. 'Yes I was, Tommy.'

'Um, Sir Benedict?' Tommy wasn't sure how to ask her next question. 'Why do Lil and the Old Wrecks and the other creatures of the castle talk to some people and not others?'

Sir Benedict looked thoughtful. 'Many things can talk, Tommy, but only to those who take the trouble to listen. And listening is a skill which can't be taught – like kindness can't be taught. I'll tell you something which can be taught, though: sword fighting. Why don't you bring Jasper out to the courtyard and I'll show you a few moves.'

Tommy thought her heart would burst with joy. It was as if all her dreams were coming true. She was the sword girl, and she was about to have a sword-fighting lesson with Sir Benedict. With a happy sigh, she drew her sword from the rack and hurried after her hero.

Join Tommy and
her friends for another
SWORD GIRL
adventure in

THE
Poison
PLOT

CHAPTER 1

'MAKE WAY, MAKE WAY! Fifty kinds of fresh fish coming through for the kitchen!'

It was early morning, and Tommy was crossing the great courtyard of Flamant Castle. She dodged out of the way of the cart clattering across the flagstones, only to hear someone behind her yell: 'Watch where you're going, girlie. I've got five hundred eggs in this basket!'

'Sorry,' Tommy said, as the egg woman barged past her.

The courtyard was busier than she'd ever seen it. She stepped out of the path of a man rolling two enormous rounds of cheese, as big as cart wheels.

'Poultry coming through: starlings, storks and swans!'

Tommy craned her head to look at the brace of birds the poultry man had slung around his neck. What was going on?

She had almost reached the armoury where she worked when she saw a small round man in brown robes. Despite all the activity in the courtyard, he was looking at the sky.

'Good morning, sir,' Tommy said to the physician.

'Eh?' said the physician. 'Oh, hello, Sword Girl. Have you seen the carrier pigeon?'

'No,' said Tommy. 'Not this morning.'

'Bother. I need some of his droppings for one of my cures.' The physician looked up at the sky again.

'Sir, why is the castle so busy this morning?' Tommy asked.

'Busy?' The physician looked around at the tradespeople hurrying to and fro. 'I suppose it must be something to do with the great banquet,' he said.

'A great banquet?' said Tommy, excited. 'What banquet?'

But the physician had wandered off. 'Where is that pigeon?' he was muttering to himself.

Maybe the blacksmith would know something about the great banquet, Tommy hoped.

She entered the armoury to see the blacksmith standing by the fire, softening a piece of armour that needed reshaping. Several shields and helmets were stacked

on the workbench, also in need of repair.

'Smith, have you heard about the great banquet?' Tommy asked.

The blacksmith looked up at her from under his bushy eyebrows. 'Oh aye, I've heard about it,' he said. 'But we've no time for feastin' here, Sword Girl. Sir Benedict and his men will be leaving tomorrow to patrol Sir Walter's lands. They'll need two dozen swords, so you'd better hop to it.'

'Yes, Smith,' said Tommy. 'Right away.' As Keeper of the Blades, it was her job to clean and sharpen all the bladed weapons of the castle.

She went through the door to the left of the fireplace into the sword chamber and quickly got to work. Pulling swords from the long rack against the wall opposite the door, she used a file and whetstone to sharpen the blades before polishing them with clove-scented oil.

'You're working hard this morning, dearie,' came a voice from a small rack of swords in the dimmest part of the room. It was one of the Old Wrecks. These were the swords that had never been carried into battle, and so were never used by the knights of Flamant Castle. They had been dusty and neglected when Tommy first started work in the sword chamber, but now their blades shone in the light of the candle flickering on the wall. What none of the knights knew – except Sir Benedict – was that the Old

Wrecks were inhabited by the spirits of their last owners.

Tommy glanced at the sabre which had spoken. 'Hello, Nursie,' she said. 'Smith told me that Sir Benedict is taking some of the knights out on a patrol tomorrow, so I have to get their swords ready.'

Sir Benedict was Flamant Castle's bravest knight, and he was responsible for the safety of the castle and lands belonging to Sir Walter the Bald and his wife, Lady Beatrix the Bored.

'A patrol, eh?' a deep voice boomed from a long-handled dagger. 'It sounds like trouble on the borders, if you ask me.'

'Well I didn't ask you, Bevan Brumm,' Nursie replied. 'What would you know about patrols? You were a merchant, not a knight.'

'I think Bevan Brumm might be right, though,' said another, younger voice. This was Jasper Swann. Jasper had been a squire, training to be a knight, before he fell ill and died. 'I heard some of the knights talking in here the other day and one of them said that Sir Malcolm the Mean had been trying to steal some of Sir Walter's land.'

'Who is Sir Malcolm the Mean?' Tommy wanted to know.

'He has the lands to the west of here,

dearie,' Nursie explained. 'But his own lands have never been enough for him. Oh no. He wants his neighbours' lands too.'

'He wants Sir Walter's lands?' exclaimed Tommy.

'Not just his lands, Sword Girl,' rumbled Bevan Brumm. 'Sir Malcolm the Mean wants Flamant Castle – and if Sir Benedict can't stop him at the border ...'

Tommy's heart started to pound. 'What?' she said. 'What will happen if Sir Benedict can't stop him?'

Bevan Brumm sounded grim. 'Flamant Castle will be at war.'

ABOUT THE AUTHOR

FRANCES WATTS was born in the medieval city of Lausanne, in Switzerland, and moved to Australia when she was three. After studying literature at university she began working as an editor. Her bestselling picture books include *Kisses for Daddy* and the 2008 Children's Book Council of Australia award-winner, *Parsley Rabbit's Book about Books* (both illustrated by David Legge). Frances is also the author of a series about two very unlikely superheroes, Extraordinary Ernie and Marvellous Maud, and the highly acclaimed children's fantasy/adventure series, the Gerander Trilogy.

Frances lives in Sydney's inner west, and divides her time between writing and editing. Her cat doesn't talk.

ABOUT THE ILLUSTRATOR

GREGORY ROGERS has always loved art and drawing so it's no surprise he became an illustrator. He was the first Australian to win the prestigious Kate Greenaway Medal. The first of his popular wordless picture book series, *The Boy, the Bear, the Baron, the Bard*, was selected as one of the Ten Best Illustrated Picture Books of 2004 by the *New York Times* and short-listed for the Children's Book Council of Australia Book of the Year Award in 2005. The third book, *The Hero of Little Street*, won the CBCA Picture Book of the Year in 2010. Gregory loves movies and music, and is a collector of books, antiques and anything odd and unusual.

He lives in Brisbane above a bookshop cafe with his cat Sybil.

Tournament
TROUBLE

'I want you to fight in the tournament, Tommy.'

Flamant Castle is having a tournament! But when one of the squires is injured during practice, Sir Benedict asks Tommy to take his place. He even offers her one of his own horses to ride. It's a dream come true for Tommy. There's just one problem: she has never ridden a horse before – and every time she tries to ride Bess, the horse throws her off! Time is running out …
How will Tommy be able to compete?

COMING IN SEPTEMBER 2012

THE *Siege* SCARE

'We're under siege!'

When Sir Walter, Sir Benedict and the other knights go to nearby Roses Castle for a tournament, the enemy knights from Malice attack Flamant. The only hope of rescue lies in getting a message to Sir Benedict, a day's ride away. But the castle is surrounded and there's no way out! With the help of her friends, Tommy devises a daring plan. Can she save Flamant Castle before it's too late?

COMING IN SEPTEMBER 2012